From my home to yours —M. R.

For Skye —E. H.

BLOOMSBURY CHILDREN'S BOOKS
Bloomsbury Publishing Inc., part of Bloomsbury Publishing Plc
1385 Broadway, New York, NY 10018

BLOOMSBURY, BLOOMSBURY CHILDREN'S BOOKS, and the Diana logo
are trademarks of Bloomsbury Publishing Plc

First published in Great Britain in September 2020 by Bloomsbury Publishing Plc
Published in the United States of America in October 2020
by Bloomsbury Children's Books

Bloomsbury books may be purchased for business or promotional use. For information on bulk purchases please contact
Macmillan Corporate and Premium Sales Department at specialmarkets@macmillan.com

Library of Congress Cataloging-in-Publication Data
available upon request
ISBN 978-1-5476-0713-6 (hardcover) · ISBN 978-1-5476-0751-8 (e-book) · ISBN 978-1-5476-0752-5 (e-PDF)

Book design by Goldy Broad · Typeset in Filosofia
Printed and bound in the United Kingdom by Bell & Bain Limited, Glasgow
2 4 6 8 10 9 7 5 3 1

All papers used by Bloomsbury Publishing Plc are natural, recyclable products made from
wood grown in well-managed forests. The manufacturing processes conform to the
environmental regulations of the country of origin.

To find out more about our authors and books visit www.bloomsbury.com
and sign up for our newsletters.

The World Made a RAINBOW

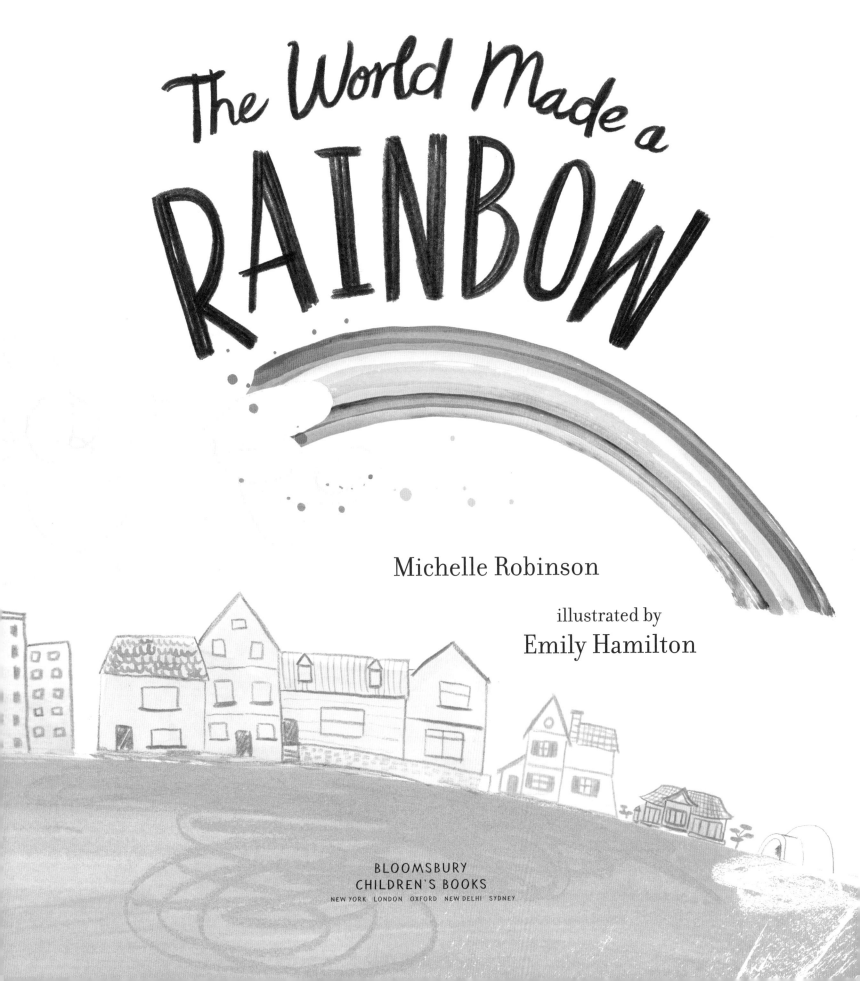

Michelle Robinson

illustrated by
Emily Hamilton

BLOOMSBURY
CHILDREN'S BOOKS

NEW YORK LONDON OXFORD NEW DELHI SYDNEY

All of the world had to stay home today.
I wished that it didn't. I wanted to play.

I missed everybody. My grandma. My friends.
My mom said, "You'll see them, once everything mends."

"Let's paint a **big rainbow** to put on display.

When people pass by it and see it, they'll say,

'All rainstorms must end,

and this rainstorm will, too.'"

"And they'll feel a bit happier, all thanks to you."

So we dig out the paint pots.

I LOVE
making
ART!

We've got lots of RED,
and so that's where I start.

But RED makes me think of
the chairs in my class . . .

Mom gives me a cuddle,
"This rainstorm will pass."

"I can't reach the ORANGE . . . !"
But Mom has to work,
And Dad's with my brother,
who's going berserk.

I'll paint with the YELLOW.
It's bright like the sun.
I spread it around with the red.

This is FUN!

I've made my own
ORANGE!

But I can't make GREEN.
I'd need BLUE for that,
but the blue paint's wiped clean.

I start to feel lonely.

I start to feel sad.

Then . . .

"How about odd bits
of cardboard?" says Dad.

He cuts, and I stick,
and my brother helps, too.
We have to mix flour and water for glue.

It looks really good . . .

"Like the ocean," says Mom.
"And all the **adventures** that we'll still go on . . ."

"The forest!"

"The park!"

"The light couldn't
SHINE
if it never knew
dark."

"And **rainbows** can't **color** the world without **rain**."

So we get back to work on my rainbow again.

I've never been quite sure what INDIGO's like!

Dad laughs. "INDIGO—

like your very first bike!"

And they dig out a memory box I've never seen,

packed with mementos

from places we've been.

I shout, "Indigo!"
as I spot my mom's jeans.
Well, I can't cut *them* out—
so we use magazines.

Then Dad takes a picture for Gram, and I say,
"Memories are good.
We'll make more every day."

My rainbow looks GREAT!

There's just

VIOLET

to go . . .

Violet, the **loveliest** person I know!

Violet's my best friend.
I miss her,
SO much.

Mom fetches her laptop.
"Let's put you in touch . . ."

And—would you believe?
Violet feels just like me,
and she's making a rainbow for people to see!

We walk to see hers,

and she walks to see mine.

We wave to each other and really, it's fine.

Not perfect—but neither's my rainbow. So what?
I'm perfectly **happy** with all that I've got.

Violet, my parents, my brother, my friends . . .

And we'll still have **each other**
when this rainstorm ends!